Richard Scarry's
Busy Day Storybooks

Humperdink's
Busy Day

J.B. COMMUNICATIONS INC.

It is very early
in the morning.

All of Busytown
is still fast asleep.

"Drrinnng!" sounds the alarm clock next to Baker Humperdink's bed.

It is time for him to begin baking bread for hungry Busytowners!

5

Baker Humperdink rides off through the dark on his bicycle to the bakery.

Brushes drives by in his street sweeper. "Good morning, Humperdink!" calls Brushes. "Good morning, Brushes!" waves Humperdink. Humperdink stops at Able Baker Charlie's house.

Able Baker Charlie hops onto Humperdink's bicycle.

On their way to the bakery, they pass
the TV bug reporters.
They are out to report the morning's
news.

7

At the bakery, Humperdink and Able Baker Charlie first warm up the oven.

While the oven gets hot, Humperdink kneads bread dough made from flour, water, salt and yeast.

Able Baker Charlie makes different-shaped loaves of bread out of the bread dough.

Good work, Charlie!

When the loaves are ready,
Humperdink and Able Baker
Charlie put them in the oven.

Now they must wait for the loaves
of bread to bake.

"What do you say we have a donut raffle today?" Humperdink asks Charlie.

Charlie agrees that it's a great idea.
He prepares the raffle tickets while
Humperdink makes the donuts.

Whoops! I think the bread is ready boys!

Humperdink and Able Baker Charlie run to the oven.

They take out the baked bread just in time.
Ummm! Doesn't it smell delicious?

While the bread cools, they put the donuts into the oven.

Once the loaves of bread have cooled, Humperdink places them in the bakery window.

Able Baker Charlie is going to make deliveries.
"Drive carefully, Charlie!" Humperdink says.

Charlie climbs onto his delivery bicycle and pedals away.

First he delivers long French baguettes to Louie's Restaurant.

"How are you today?" Louie asks Charlie. "Very well, thank you!" replies Able Baker Charlie.

Charlie then brings bread to Hank's market.

"Have a nice day, Charlie!" says Hank. "Thanks, Hank!" says Charlie, pedaling away.

When Able Baker Charlie returns to the bakery, he sees the firefighters going inside.

"Have they come to buy some bread?" wonders Charlie.

NO! They have come to put out a burnt-donut fire! "Whooosh!" goes the firefighters' water hose.

When the fire is out, the firefighters leave the bakery.

"Don't forget to take a raffle ticket!" Humperdink says.

Humperdink starts to make a new batch of donuts.

Just then, Patience, the baby-sitter, arrives with little Sophie Humperdink.
"Could you please look after Sophie while I go to my dental appointment?" Patience asks Humperdink.
"No problem, Patience!" Humperdink says.

Both Humperdink and Able Baker Charlie are a little tired from getting up so early in the morning.

They decide to have a nap while the new donuts bake in the oven.

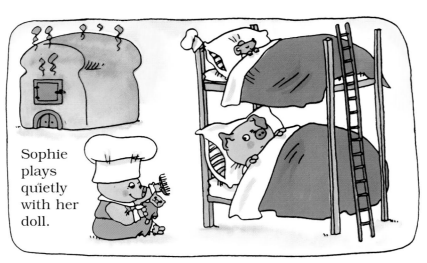

Sophie
plays
quietly
with her
doll.

Suddenly,
Humperdink is
awakened by
a strange noise.

Oh no! It's the firefighters again!

Humperdink and Able Baker
Charlie leap from their beds and take
the baked donuts out of the oven
just in time!

Good work, boys!

Now it is time for the raffle!
Humperdink reaches into his hat
to pull out the winning number.

He pulls out a ticket
and holds it up.

"The winning ticket..."
shouts Charlie,
"is number four!"

"That's OUR ticket!" says Smokey.
"We won the raffle!"

Baker Humperdink and Able Baker Charlie
bring out the big raffle prize.
The firefighters look very pleased.
They love to eat donuts.

The firefighters drive away with their prize.
"You know, Charlie," says Humperdink, "we haven't eaten a *thing* all day!"
They decide to have a good meal at Louie's Restaurant.

... a big bowl of breadcrumb soup!

Their favorite!